The American Girls

1764

Kaya, an adventurous Nez Perce girl whose deep love for horses and respect for nature nourish her spirit

1774

Felicity, a spunky, spritely colonial girl, full of energy and independence

1824

Josefina, an Hispanic girl whose heart and hopes are as big as the New Mexico sky

1854

Kirsten, a pioneer girl of strength and spirit who settles on the frontier

1864

Addy, a courageous girl determined to be free in the midst of the Civil War

1904

Samantha, a bright Victorian beauty, an orphan raised by her wealthy grandmother

1934

Kit, a clever, resourceful girl facing the Great Depression with spirit and determination

1944

Molly, who schemes and dreams on the home front during World War Two

1764

Kaya Shows the Way

A Sister Story

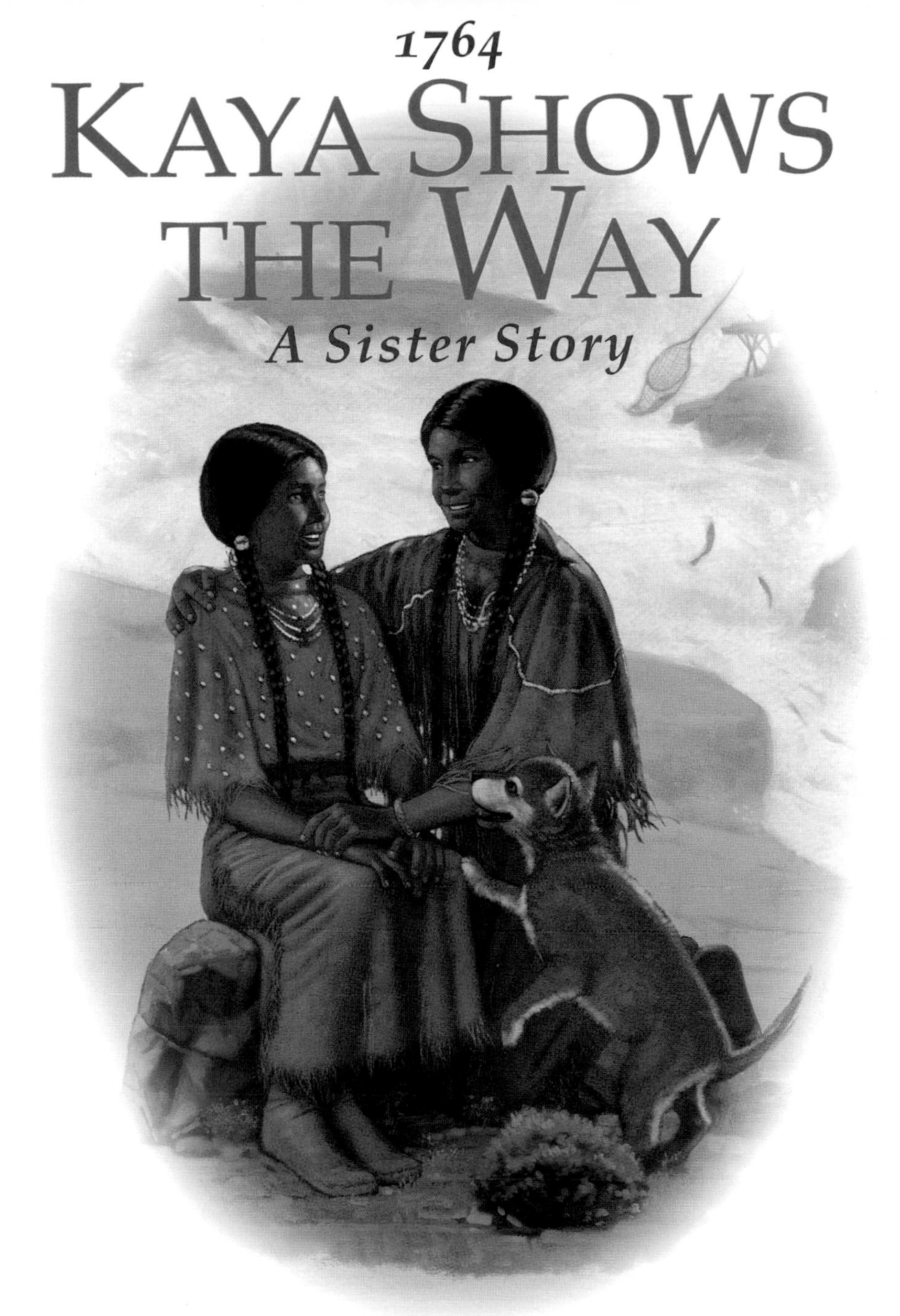

By Janet Shaw

Illustrations Bill Farnsworth

Vignettes Susan McAliley

American Girl

Published by Pleasant Company Publications

For information, address: Book Editor, Pleasant Company Publications, 8400 Fairway Place, P.O. Box 620998, Middleton, WI 53562.

Visit our Web site at **americangirl.com**

Printed in China.
02 03 04 05 06 07 08 LEO 12 11 10 9 8 7 6 5 4 3 2

PICTURE CREDITS
The following individuals and organizations have generously given permission to reprint images contained in "Looking Back":

pp. 66–67— photograph by Hiromi Naito from the book *Sockeye Salmon* (salmon swimming); photo by Archie W. McKeown (woman cooking salmon); photo by Wilma Roberts (salmon cooking); Library of Congress (historical photo of dip-netting); photo by Wilma Roberts (contemporary photo of dip-netting); pp. 68–69— The Smithsonian Institution Bureau of American Ethnicity (neg. 2977) (tepees and shields); Northwest Museum of Arts & Culture/Eastern Washington State Historical Society, Spokane (horse collar); University of Pennsylvania Museum (neg. #T4-791c) (Shinny stick); Washington State University Libraries (women playing Stick Game); pp. 70–71— Nez Perce National Historical Park (NEPE-HI-3392) (courting couple); Idaho State Historical Society (courting flute); The Smithsonian Institution National Museum of Natural History (NMNH #213523) (doll); photo by Wilma Roberts (Celilo Falls); © Kevin Fleming/CORBIS (salmon jumping upstream).

Library of Congress Cataloging-in-Publication Data

Cataloging-in-Publication Data available from Library of Congress

TO MY STEPDAUGHTER, BETSY,
AND TED, WITH LOVE.

Kaya and her family are *Nimíipuu*, known today as Nez Perce Indians. They speak the Nez Perce language, so you'll see some Nez Perce words in this book. Kaya is short for the Nez Perce name *Kaya'aton'my'*, which means "she who arranges rocks." You'll find the meanings and pronunciations of these and other Nez Perce words in the glossary on page 72.

Table of Contents

TOE-TA
Kaya's father, an expert horseman and wise village leader.

EETSA
Kaya's mother, who is a good provider for her family and her village.

KAYA
An adventurous girl with a generous spirit.

BROWN DEER
Kaya's sister, who is old enough to court.

WING FEATHER AND SPARROW
Kaya's mischievous twin brothers.

. . . AND FRIENDS

WHITE BRAIDS
A kind woman who saves Speaking Rain's life.

SPEAKING RAIN
A blind girl who lives with Kaya's family and is a sister to her.

PI-LAH-KA AND KAUTSA
Eetsa's parents, who guide and comfort Kaya.

TWO HAWKS
A Salish boy who is a friend to Kaya.

CHAPTER
ONE

THE SOUND OF THE FALLS

Long before Kaya could see the waterfalls on the river ahead, she began to hear their voices. She and her family were riding over hot, dry plains, so the murmur of running water was a sweet promise. But as they rode closer to the river, that murmur grew into a powerful song, like many men drumming. When the riders crested the last hill and looked down at the shining river, Kaya saw the falls plunging over black cliffs. Even at this distance the falls roared like thunder. The earth seemed to tremble.

Kaya's little brother Wing Feather was seated behind Kaya on the chestnut horse. He held her tightly around the waist. "Is that a monster roaring?" he asked in a small voice.

Kaya patted his leg. "That's the sound of the falls you hear," she said. "Remember when we stayed here last summer? Remember how you and Sparrow played all day with your cousins, and there were games and races every night? And remember how many salmon gave themselves to all the fishermen?"

Wing Feather only hugged her more tightly, one hand tucked into his baby moccasin. Kaya knew he was trying to be strong, but the roar of Celilo Falls frightened many children.

"The water sounds angry!" Sparrow said. He was riding behind Kaya's older sister, Brown Deer.

"But the river's our friend, and you'll soon get used to its roar," Brown Deer said. Her voice was calm, but her cheeks were flushed with excitement. Kaya knew her sister was eager to meet family and friends here at the falls. Brown Deer would also meet Cut Cheek again, whom she hoped to marry.

Kaya's father, who rode ahead, signaled for everyone to halt before beginning the steep descent from the bluffs into the valley. He and other men and women dismounted and began checking the heavy packs to make sure they were tied tightly and wouldn't slip and injure a horse or rider.

Kaya dismounted and gazed down at the vast river valley. Stony islands clustered in the river, white water sweeping around them. Kaya saw large horse herds grazing on the flatlands. Many fishing platforms of sticks lashed together had been built out over the water. Hundreds of tepees and lodges lined both shores as far upstream and downstream as she could see. The villages were those of many different peoples—some who lived on the river all year and others who visited from the plains, the mountains, and the ocean to fish and trade. Kaya's band, and many other bands of *Nimíipuu*, were joining them for the yearly return of salmon up the Big River.

Kaya shaded her eyes and peered at the mist that rose like thick smoke from the waterfalls. She saw bright rainbows arching low over the falls, and her heart lifted. Rainbows were good signs. She hoped to meet up with her friend Two Hawks here at the falls. He'd said that when they met again, he might have good news of Kaya's sister, Speaking Rain. When she and Two Hawks had escaped from their enemies, they'd had to leave Speaking Rain behind.

But Kaya knew that Two Hawks might be bringing bad news instead. He might have learned that Speaking Rain had been abandoned by their captors—or injured, or lost. For how could a blind girl get along without someone to care for her?

As if Tatlo sensed Kaya's troubled thoughts, the pup bounded up to her, his pink tongue hanging out. He was growing fast, and his legs were getting long. Kaya bent and put her face against his soft ear. "You'll help me find my sister, won't you?" she whispered to him. He licked her hand, his tail wagging in circles, as if he were saying, *I'll try.*

Kaya's grandmother climbed off her horse and began adjusting the travois on a pack horse. When *Kautsa* saw the twins' worried frowns, her lined face softened. "*Aa-heh*, the falls are hissing and raging, boys," she said, "but that's because they're so steep and so wide. Don't you remember how Coyote made them for us?" She turned to Kaya. "Would you comfort your brothers with that story while I fix this travois?"

"Aa-heh," Kaya said quickly. Each day she reminded herself to do her very best. She wanted to be trustworthy like her friend Swan Circling, the warrior woman who'd given Kaya her name to use when she was older.

Wing Feather and Sparrow slid off the horses. "Tell about Coyote!" Sparrow begged her.

"Tell about his tricks!" Wing Feather added. Everyone loved stories about Coyote, who was always playing tricks and teaching lessons at the same time.

Kaya sat with the twins on a travois, and Tatlo, panting, lay down in the shade at their feet. "One day Coyote was coming up the river," she began. "And in those long-ago days the river was calm, because the River People had dammed it up—they wanted to keep all the salmon for themselves. Coyote was hot and tired, like we are, and he decided to swim in the cool water. He swam around until he saw five beautiful river girls on the shore. He saw a chance to play a trick on the River People, so he turned himself into a baby and came floating over the water toward the girls."

"I remember what Coyote did then!" Wing Feather cried. "He bawled like a baby—*Wah! Wah!*—to get the girls' attention!"

"Aa-heh," Kaya said. "He cried, and the girls quickly swam out to pull him from the water. 'What a precious baby!' they said. But the youngest sister wasn't fooled. 'Watch out!' she said. 'That's no baby. That's Coyote!' The baby put out his lower lip as if he was about to cry again. 'Don't tease him,' the other girls said. 'Let's take him home with us.'

"The girls fed the baby and took care of him, and he grew fast. One day he spilled a cup of water. 'Get me more water!' he demanded. The youngest sister, who still didn't trust the baby, said, 'Let's make him get water himself.' So the baby began to crawl toward the river. When he was out of sight, he jumped up and ran. 'He certainly moves fast!' one of the girls said. The youngest sister said, 'That's because he's Coyote!'

"I know what happened next!" Sparrow cried. "Coyote broke down the fish dam that the River People had made!"

"Aa-heh, Coyote swam up to their fish dam and tore it down, pulling out all the stones so the water rushed free over the falls," Kaya continued. "He jumped up and down on the stones and shouted gleefully, 'Look, your fish dam is broken!' The girls saw that it was so. The youngest sister said, 'I told you he was Coyote!'

"Coyote said to them, 'You selfishly kept all the salmon behind your dam. But now the salmon will be able to swim upstream to spawn. People will be happy because they can catch the fish, and they'll thank me for giving them food.' And that's how Celilo Falls came to be, and why salmon can swim up all the rivers and streams now," Kaya finished.

"Did Coyote really make those waterfalls?" Sparrow asked, pointing at the water rushing over black stones. Because he was thinking about the story, he was no longer frightened.

"You can see for yourself that the fish dam's not

there anymore," Kaya said with a smile. "And who else but Coyote could have knocked it down so that the salmon could swim upstream?"

She scratched Tatlo behind his ears and gazed at the distant hills across the river. Would Two Hawks and his people soon be riding over those hills? Would she be strong no matter what news he brought of Speaking Rain? And what of her beloved horse—would she discover Steps High in one of the many horse herds here at the falls?

"*Katsee-yow-yow* for telling the story," Kautsa said. "Come along now. We're ready to move on."

After Kaya and the others greeted friends and relatives, the women set up their tepees and unpacked their goods. Then *Eetsa* gave Kaya permission to join the other girls, all of whom were like cousins to her. Some girls had gathered on a flat stretch of ground to play a stickball game called Shinny. They'd formed two teams and were chasing a rawhide ball, hitting it to each other with curved sticks. As Kaya walked up, several of the girls waved to her.

"Play on our side, Kaya!" Little Fawn called to her. "You're a fast runner!"

"Play on our side!" Rabbit called. "Magpies fly fast!"

Magpie, again! As Kaya picked up a shinny stick, she tried to shrug off that awful nickname she'd gotten when she had neglected her brothers and all the children had been switched because of her forgetfulness. And as soon as she was running down the field with the others, she forgot about everything except the game. The girls batted the ball and passed it to each other, trying to hit it between two branches stuck in the ground at each end of the playing field. Some dogs, barking wildly, ran along with them.

Little Fawn knocked the ball to Kaya, and she raced down the field with it, Tatlo right at her heels. But when other girls charged after Kaya, Tatlo got caught in the middle of the action. Someone stepped on his paw, and, with a yelp, he tumbled head over heels. Kaya stopped playing and led her pup to the sidelines.

Rabbit was there, tying her moccasins more tightly. "*Tawts-may-we,* cousin!" she greeted Kaya.

*Little Fawn knocked the ball to Kaya,
and she raced down the field with it, Tatlo right at her heels.*

"Tawts-may-we! Have you been here at the river long?" Kaya stroked Tatlo's ears as she caught her breath.

"Not long," Rabbit said. "Only for two sleeps."

"I want to find Two Hawks," Kaya said. "Have you seen him?"

"Raven went looking for him yesterday," Rabbit said. "He told us that no Salish people have come here yet. They don't always make the long journey, you know."

"I know," Kaya admitted. Two Hawks had given his promise, but his people might have made different plans. Her heart sank when she thought that he might not be able to bring her news of Speaking Rain after all.

"Your pup runs fast," Rabbit said, holding out her hand for Tatlo to sniff. "But I think his rear legs run faster than his front legs!"

"Aa-heh," Kaya said. "I'm going to tie him by our tepee so he won't get trampled."

"Come back quickly!" Rabbit called after her.

When Kaya approached her tepee, an elderly, gray-haired woman Kaya didn't recognize was carrying her belongings inside. Brown Deer knelt by a travois, untying more rolls of tule mats. She beckoned for Kaya to come close. "Cut Cheek's parents have sent one of his aunts to live with us for a while," she said in a low voice. "Crane Song's here to make sure I'm a strong worker and will make a good wife for Cut Cheek." She looked pleased, but she seemed nervous as well.

"Everyone knows you're a strong worker!" Kaya assured her sister, who was so dutiful and so good.

Brown Deer shook her head. "A woman has to prove her worth," she said softly.

"You'll be a fine wife for Cut Cheek. His aunt will see that right away," Kaya insisted. She tied one end of a piece of cord around Tatlo's neck and the other end to one of the tepee stakes.

Brown Deer frowned. "Tie Tatlo farther away, will you? Sometimes he chews on the tepee coverings, and I won't have time to look after him."

Kaya led Tatlo to a stack of tepee poles and tied him there. He sat with his ears drooping, whining as if he were being punished.

"Katsee-yow-yow, Kaya," Brown Deer said gratefully. She picked up the mats and hurried into the tepee, where Crane Song waited for her.

Kaya patted Tatlo on his rump. "Don't whine," she told him. "I'll be back for you soon."

At the beginning of each new run of salmon, everyone honored and thanked the fish with a feast. Kautsa and the other women built big, slow-burning fires to roast the salmon. While the fish cooked under the open sky, the women spread rows of tule mats down the center of a lodge large enough to seat all their family and friends. Kaya stood with the other girls and women across from the men and boys while her grandfather led them in prayer.

"*Hun-ya-wat* made this earth," *Pi-lah-ka* said. "He made all living things on the earth, in the water, and in the sky. He made Nimíipuu and all peoples. He created food for all His creatures. We respect and give thanks for His creations."

All the people took a sip of water to purify their bodies before they accepted the gifts from the Creator. After everyone had taken a sip of the cold river water, each person took a tiny bite of salmon, giving thanks before beginning the rest of the meal.

The men and boys served the roasted meat they'd

provided. The women and girls brought forward the foods they'd gathered. With the others, Kaya placed bowls filled with roots and berries on the mats. Then the women brought large wooden bowls of the cooked salmon into the lodge.

Kaya watched Brown Deer moving quickly and quietly along the mats. It was a great honor to feed the others, and Brown Deer kept her eyes downcast, even when she offered Cut Cheek a bowl. But her face reddened slightly when he took it from her.

Surely Crane Song will see what a fine woman Brown Deer is, Kaya thought. And soon Cut Cheek would prove his worth by fishing well and bravely with the other men. If their parents approved, the couple could marry in the autumn.

That thought made Kaya's heart glad—and also sad. She wanted Brown Deer to marry Cut Cheek, but she was sad to think of her sister leaving their family. She'd lost one sister when she'd had to leave Speaking Rain with the enemies. Now she felt she might be losing her other sister as well.

CHAPTER
TWO

DANGEROUS CROSSING!

When Kaya followed her mother and the other women to the riverbank the next morning, the men and boys were already fishing. Some spearfished from rocky outcroppings along the shore. Others stood on sturdy poles lashed together to make platforms built out over the falls. They held their long-handled dip nets down into the crashing waters. When a salmon leaped into a dip net, the force of the current closed the net around it. But it took great strength to lift a large, struggling fish, and if a man was pulled into the rushing water, he could be swept over the falls and drowned. For safety, the men tied lines around their waists and secured the lines to rocks. Kaya shivered as she saw *Toe-ta* and the others leaning over the raging waters.

The men's work was difficult and dangerous, but the women and girls worked hard, too. All day Kaya helped carry the heavy salmon the men caught to the women who cleaned the fish and sliced them into thin strips. Other women hung the strips on racks, to be dried by the sun and wind. By the end of the day, Kaya's hands, arms, and back ached.

As Kaya walked with Kautsa to their village upstream above the falls, she wiped her eyes with a handful of soft grass. "The wind makes my eyes sting," she said.

"Aa-heh," Kautsa said, wiping her own eyes. "The wind blowing up the gorge is a powerful force! But it's another gift from Hun-ya-wat. With so much wind, fish dry very quickly. There's no need to build drying fires here at the falls."

Kaya looked back down the valley at the villages that crowded the shore. "I've been watching for Salish people to arrive," she said. "Two Hawks might come with them."

"They could be on the other side of the river,"

Kautsa said. "Two women came across today in a canoe to trade with us. I don't speak their language, but Crane Song knows it. The traders told her that newcomers from the north were putting up tepees over there."

Kaya felt a shiver of hope. "Did they say anything about a blind girl?"

"About our Speaking Rain?" Kautsa asked. "If they had, I'd have taken a canoe to see for myself! But they said only that the newcomers had hide-covered tepees, not like ours."

"Two Hawks' people have hide tepees!" Kaya said. "Couldn't I cross the river with the traders and see who the newcomers are? I could cross back later with some fishermen."

Kautsa looked kindly into Kaya's eyes. "I know you won't be satisfied until you see for yourself," she said. "The traders tied their canoe upstream. Surely they'll have room for you. Take them some finger cakes as a gift."

Kaya ran to their camping place, where Brown Deer was sweeping the ground with a broom of sage branches. Her older sister looked tired and unhappy.

"Is something wrong?" Kaya asked.

"I think something's wrong with *me*," Brown Deer admitted. "I'm doing my very best to please Crane Song. I was the first one to waken, long before first light. I brought fresh water and built up the fire before she'd even stirred. Still, all she did was frown and shake her head as though I'm not working hard enough."

"You've always been hardworking and respectful," Kaya insisted. "And you're strong and good, too."

"I'm trying my very best," Brown Deer said. "I don't think my best is good enough for Crane Song."

"But of all the girls, Cut Cheek chose you!" Kaya said, her face hot with feeling. "And you chose him, too! That means more than anything, doesn't it?"

"It does to us," Brown Deer said. "But if Crane Song isn't convinced I'll make a good wife, Cut Cheek's family won't approve of our marriage."

Kaya couldn't believe what she was hearing. All her life she'd admired her older sister, and she feared she would never be as steady or as strong as Brown Deer. "What does Kautsa say about this?" she asked.

"Kautsa says these things take time," Brown Deer said. "She says to be patient, that Crane Song might seem hard-hearted, but she's fair. What do you think, Kaya?"

"I think Kautsa's wise in all things," Kaya said. "You can trust her judgment."

"I hope so," Brown Deer said. "Everything depends on Crane Song's good opinion of me." She set aside the broom and got her knife and workbag. "I've finished cleaning here," she said. "Now I have to join her. Wish me well, Sister." Walking fast, she took the path toward where the women were cutting up salmon and spreading the strips onto drying racks.

Kaya ran into their tepee and put a handful of kouse cakes into the bag she wore on her belt. Then she had an idea. She took Speaking Rain's doll from her pack and tucked it into her belt. If, somehow, she found her sister, she wanted to put the beloved doll into her arms—a sign that she'd never lost hope they'd be together again.

Tatlo was sleeping in the shade beside the tepee. When Kaya came out with the doll, she crouched and he jumped up and licked her chin.

Then he sniffed the doll and licked it, too.

"Do you want to come with me?" Kaya asked. Tatlo barked twice, as if saying Aa-heh! He ran ahead as she raced up the shore to where two women were putting bundles into a dugout cedar canoe.

Kaya threw the elder woman the words, *May I cross the river with you?*

With her hands, the elder woman said, *Come with us.*

Gratefully, Kaya gave her the kouse cakes and climbed into the canoe, with Tatlo jumping in right behind.

The young woman knelt in the prow of the canoe, and the elder woman sat in the stern. The elder woman expertly guided the canoe away from shore. Soon they were paddling across a place where the water was shallower and quieter than the rest of the river. This was a prized fishing place because it was easy to see salmon in the clear, smoothly running water. A fisherman could slip his net over a large fish, just like roping a horse.

Kaya saw the boys Raven and Fox Tail fishing together on a little island just downstream.

They'd tied their safety lines around the same rock, and they were taking turns using a big dip net. As Kaya watched, Raven dragged up the net with a large salmon twisting in it. Fox Tail helped him hold the long, heavy pole until they got the netted fish onto the rocks. Raven took his fish club and killed the salmon with a single blow. Kaya could see it was a good catch.

The many fish leaping and splashing around the canoe excited Tatlo. He put his feet up on the side and barked at them. "Get down!" Kaya said. "Down!" She grabbed the big pup by the scruff of his neck and tried to make him sit. But Tatlo was too excited to sit. When a salmon jumped right next to the canoe, he lunged and snapped at it—and toppled out of the canoe into the river! The surging current caught him and swept him downstream.

"Help my dog!" Kaya cried. The wind whipped her braids across her face and tore away her words. She watched in horror as Tatlo struggled to swim in the churning river. His paws thrashed the water, and his amber eyes looked about wildly. Each time he came up for air, the current dragged him under again. Surely he'd be swept down to the falls and

"Help my dog!" Kaya cried.

killed on the rocks below!

The elder woman turned the canoe downstream, and the young woman paddled hard and fast. But Kaya knew there was no way they could catch up to Tatlo. Already the current had carried him downstream almost to the island.

Then she saw Raven looking their way. He quickly thrust the dip net back into the river. Fox Tail leaned out and peered down into the wild water. Then, with a sweep, Raven raised the net with something in it. Fox Tail grabbed the handle, too, and steadied the heavy weight against his body as he helped lift the net. It took a long moment for Kaya to realize that it was Tatlo they lifted out of the swirling water!

The elder woman guided the canoe toward the island. By the time they beached on the stones, the boys had Tatlo out of the net and onto his feet. The pup was coughing water and shaking it from his coat. His legs were wobbly, but he managed to wag his tail when Kaya scrambled from the canoe and knelt by him, pressing her face against his drenched head.

"The current carried him right to us!" Raven yelled over the river noise.

Then Fox Tail leaned toward Kaya with a sly grin. He put his mouth near her ear and shouted, "Magpies don't know how to take care of dogs!"

That awful nickname again! *But he's right,* she thought. *I didn't take care of Tatlo. I should have held him every moment. It's my fault he fell in.* Instead of hanging her head, she looked Fox Tail right in the eye and flapped her arms like a magpie. They both started laughing.

"Katsee-yow-yow!" she shouted so the boys could hear her thanks. With Tatlo shivering against her legs, she climbed back into the canoe so that they could continue on to the opposite shore.

Kaya made her way through the many villages crowded along the shore. She saw people from the coast trading dried shellfish, shell beads, cedar-root baskets, and canoes. People from the south had brought bowls of black stone and baskets of water-lily seeds to trade. And the people who lived in the midlands, like Kaya's people, traded elk and buffalo robes, kouse and camas cakes, and horses. But Kaya wasn't interested in the trading. She had only one thing on her mind—finding the newcomers from the north.

Tatlo stayed right by her side, his nose twitching at all the new scents around them. If any of the dogs that roamed about came too close to Kaya, a growl rose in his throat and his ears went back. He was such a loyal friend—how terrible if he had drowned because she hadn't kept him in the canoe! "I'll take better care of you," she said, patting his shoulder.

Kaya's ears buzzed with all the different languages she heard. From time to time she stopped where women were cooking and threw them the words, *Where are the newcomers camped?* Always they pointed east, so she kept walking upstream. At last she saw several hide-covered tepees ringed in a small circle. Women were building fires and carrying bundles into the tepees. Could these be Two Hawks' people? She ran, with Tatlo loping at her side.

A young woman was unloading deerskin bags from a travois. Kaya threw her the words, *What tribe are you?*

The young woman cocked her head and studied Kaya closely. She signed, *I am Salish. What tribe are you?*

Kaya swept her hand from her ear down across her chin, the sign for Nimíipuu. *Is Two Hawks with you?* she signed. *He wintered with our people.*

Two Hawks told us about you, the young woman signed. *Right now he's fishing with the men.* She motioned for Kaya to follow her to where women were putting up another tepee.

A white-haired woman with a bent back was smoothing the elk-skin tepee covering. A round-faced younger woman was pounding tepee stakes into the ground. As Kaya and the Salish woman approached these women, Tatlo sniffed the air a moment, then bounded away and began ranging back and forth between the tepees. "Tatlo! Come!" Kaya called, wanting to keep him close to her. When he didn't come, she ran after him.

Horses grazed near the tepees. Tatlo ran between them, his tail wagging, and headed for some small pines. Kaya followed. She saw a baby in a *tee-kas* propped against one of the pines. Tatlo was sniffing the girl who sat tending the baby. The girl's back was to Kaya, who was so intent on catching her pup that she didn't realize until she was only a few steps away that the girl was Speaking Rain!

"Sister! My sister!" Kaya cried. She felt tears sting her eyes as she went to her knees in front of Speaking Rain and seized her hand. "You're alive!"

"Kaya?" Speaking Rain hesitantly touched Kaya's face, then threw her arms around her shoulders. "Aa-heh, I'm alive! How did you find me?"

"I didn't find you," Kaya said. "My dog did! Tatlo knows your scent from your doll." She took the doll from her belt and placed it in Speaking Rain's lap. "I mended it for you and kept it safe. I knew we'd be together again!"

Speaking Rain clutched her doll to her chest, her smile shining like sun on the water. "Katsee-yow-yow," she said softly. "I prayed for you every day."

"And I prayed for you," Kaya said. As she spoke, she looked closely at her sister. When Kaya had last seen her, Speaking Rain had been thin and frail and dirty. Now she wore a fine buckskin dress decorated with many beads and elk's teeth. Her cheeks were round, and her glossy hair was sleekly braided and tied with abalone-shell ties. She wore a pretty necklace of white clamshell beads. "Two Hawks' people have been good to you, haven't they?" Kaya said.

"Aa-heh, they've been very good to me," Speaking Rain said.

Tatlo was gazing intently up at Speaking Rain, as though he recognized her. Kaya placed her sister's hand on his head. "Tatlo likes you. He's a smart dog, but even if he hadn't sniffed you out, I'd have found you."

"If Two Hawks didn't find you first!" Speaking Rain said. "He told me he was going to cross the river to look for you at sunup."

Kaya took a deep breath. "Brown Deer will be so excited to see you! Our parents will be so glad to have you with us again!"

Speaking Rain's face sobered. "I have so much to tell you," she said. "But I smell rain in the air, and don't you hear the wind rising? A storm is coming, and I should take the baby inside. Help me, and we'll talk more later."

Chapter Three

Stranded by the Storm

Kaya remembered that storms here on the Big River were often fierce ones. She picked up the baby and hurried with Speaking Rain toward the women, where the baby's mother took him and carried him into her tepee. The wind quickly grew wilder. As the sky blackened, other women rushed to bring their belongings and coals for the fires inside. Tatlo whined, wanting to follow Kaya, then huddled up with the other dogs, his head buried in his tail.

The white-haired woman led the girls to her tepee. When they were inside, she fastened the tepee flaps securely against the gusts. The woman was plump-cheeked and very old, her shoulders bent as if she were carrying a heavy load. She unrolled an elk hide and motioned for Kaya to sit on it. Then she led Speaking Rain to the hide, and spoke quietly with her. Kaya was surprised to realize that Speaking Rain spoke Salish now.

"I told White Braids that you're my sister," Speaking Rain said to Kaya. "She's the one who found me and saved my life."

Thank you for saving my sister! Kaya signed to White Braids.

You are welcome here with us, White Braids signed to Kaya. Then she poured water from a rawhide bag into a cooking basket, and set about heating stones in the fire so that she could cook with them.

Kaya leaned close to Speaking Rain. "Tell me what happened after I escaped and left you behind," Kaya urged her. "Many times I've thought how hard it must have been for you. I should never have gone!"

"But I wanted you to go!" Speaking Rain insisted. She held her doll tightly. "I *couldn't* have kept up with you. Two Hawks told us how difficult your journey was."

Pelting rain began to drive against the tepee covering. "This storm reminds me of the night I escaped," Kaya said. "Was Otter Woman angry when she discovered I was gone? Did she whip you for helping me get away?"

"She was angry, but she didn't whip me," Speaking Rain said. "They were all hurrying to pack up and break camp. They wanted to get back to their own country before snow stranded them."

"Somehow you got away from them, too," Kaya said. "Or did they abandon you?"

Speaking Rain put her hand on Kaya's arm. "I don't know what happened, Sister. I found my way to the river to drink and wash. When I came back, everyone was gone. Maybe in their rush they forgot about me. I was alone."

"My poor sister!" Kaya breathed. "What did you do?"

"I tried to stay calm," Speaking Rain said. "I needed a place to sleep, to hide. I crawled through the thicket near the river until I found grass trampled where deer had bedded down. Low branches sheltered the nest. I decided to stay there. Even if I could have found a trail, I'd never have been able to follow it."

"Did you have any food?" Kaya asked.

"They'd taken all the food," Speaking Rain said. "I tried to eat grass, but I couldn't keep it down. After a few sleeps, I was so weak that I could scarcely walk. And the nights grew colder and colder."

As Kaya listened to her sister's story, her heart hurt in her chest. "You must have been frightened," she said softly.

"I knew I would die, so I tried to make my spirit strong," Speaking Rain said. "But I drifted in and out of swirling dreams—awake, asleep? I didn't know anymore. Then I heard steps in the grass, steady ones—not a deer browsing. Someone was walking nearby. I moaned. The steps came closer, and then I felt a touch on my cheek."

"White Braids found you there?" Kaya said.

"Aa-heh," Speaking Rain said. "She was with a small group returning north. She'd come to the river to get driftwood for a fire."

"What happened after she found you?" Kaya asked.

"For a long time I was sick—coughing, choking,"

Speaking Rain said. "Each breath burned, and my face flamed. White Braids brewed *wapalwaapal* for my fever. Every day she carried me into a sweat lodge and bathed me. She fed me broth, then mush. She treated me as if I were her own child, and slowly I got stronger. When the digging season came, I was able to travel with her to the root fields. That's where Two Hawks and his family found me."

A sudden gust of wind forced smoke back inside the tepee. Squinting, White Braids fanned the smoke away from Speaking Rain, then went back to tending the fire. When the stones were hot, she dropped them into the basket of water and added pieces of salmon to boil.

"When White Braids was a young woman, she had a daughter," Speaking Rain said. "But her little girl died. White Braids says that now she has a second daughter—me. I sleep by her side and warm her. When her shoulders ache, I rub them. I carry bundles of firewood for her. She trades the hemp cord I make for hides and other things we need."

"You've cared for White Braids, just as she's cared for you," Kaya said. "Who will help her now that we've found you again?"

Speaking Rain pressed her fist to her lips. Then she took Kaya's hand in hers. "Listen to me," she said slowly, as if she'd thought through carefully what she wanted to say. "It's true that White Braids brought me here to join my family again. But, Kaya, when she saved my life, I made a vow that I'd never, ever leave her. I can't break that vow. I can never live with you again."

Kaya couldn't make sense of what she heard. Speaking Rain was back, she was safe—but she could never live with them again? "Why do you say that?" Her voice trembled with disbelief. "Eetsa and Toe-ta have been so sad! Brown Deer missed you terribly, and so did the twins. You're my sister! You must come back to us!"

Speaking Rain leaned closer and squeezed Kaya's hand harder. "Please, try to understand," she said. "When White Braids gave me back my life, I vowed I'd repay her. It was a solemn vow, Sister, and I won't break it. I know in my heart this is right."

Kaya stared at her sister's serious face. She didn't believe what she was hearing—no, she couldn't believe that she had found her sister only to lose her again! "Surely White Braids won't let you give up your family," Kaya said. "She lost her own daughter—she knows how sad your mother would be to lose you."

"I haven't told her yet that I'll never leave her," Speaking Rain admitted. "But I'm sure she'll respect my vow."

White Braids took the fish from the cooking basket with tongs and divided it into two bowls made of horn. She placed one bowl in Speaking Rain's hands and gave the other one to Kaya.

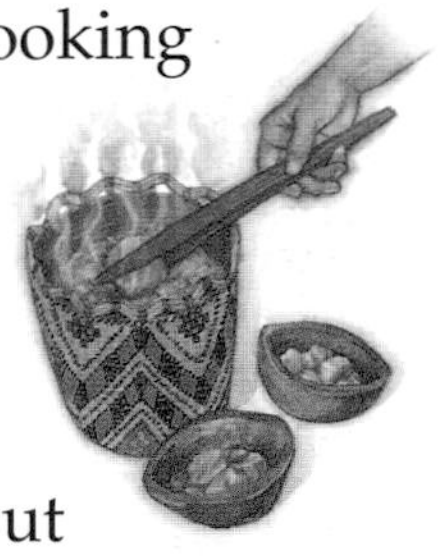

Kaya tried to eat the delicious food, but her mouth was so dry, she couldn't swallow. Her thoughts whirled like smoke in the wind. She wanted her sister back, but how could she convince Speaking Rain that it was best to be with her own family? And was it right to urge her sister to break her solemn vow?

Someone was at the doorway. White Braids unfastened the flaps and pulled them aside. It was Two Hawks. In a burst of rain he came, drenched, into the tepee, and he started when he saw Kaya. "*Tawts*, you're here!" he said. "You see, I did what

I promised. I found your sister!"

"Aa-heh, you did as you said." Kaya was more grateful than she could say, and she was proud of him, too.

A powerful-looking man followed Two Hawks inside. He and the boy dried and warmed themselves with deer hides. Then, because Two Hawks could speak both languages, he acted as an interpreter. He told Kaya that the man was his father and that his mother had stayed behind in their own country. Then he told his father that Kaya was the girl who had fled with him over the Buffalo Trail.

Two Hawks' father put his hand on Kaya's shoulder. With Two Hawks interpreting, he told her he was grateful to her and her people. He wanted to greet her parents and unite them with their lost daughter again.

As Kaya listened, she thought, *They don't know Speaking Rain has decided not to come back to us. Though she sounds so sure, maybe she has her own doubts.*

Again Kaya thanked Two Hawks and his father. Then she asked if they'd seen her horse in any of their herds.

"No one has seen your horse yet," Two Hawks said. "But someone will have Nimíipuu horses—and yours. Don't give up hope."

"I'll try to keep hoping," Kaya said, keeping her voice steady. But could she?

Two Hawks' father spoke to him again.

"My father says you must stay with us tonight," Two Hawks told Kaya. "No one can take a canoe across the river in a storm like this. When it's over, my father will find some fishermen to take you to the other side."

Kaya didn't want to stay—she wanted to take her sister back to her own people. Once Speaking Rain was with them, she'd realize that it was right. But Kaya had no choice.

White Braids served the men the food she'd prepared, then sat down beside Speaking Rain. From time to time she removed a small bone from Speaking Rain's bowl of fish, or gave her more mashed berries.

After their meal, White Braids took out the fishing net she was mending and gave Speaking Rain shredded hemp to make cord. For a while they worked quietly. Speaking Rain kept an even tension on the strands of hemp as she rolled them together into a long cord. Kaya marveled at how expert Speaking Rain had become—her cord was smooth and strong. Praising her work, White Braids patted her shoulder.

As Kaya watched them work, her own feelings were as tightly twisted as the cord. She saw that her sister wasn't just helping White Braids—the old woman relied on her now in a way that Kaya and her family never had. It came to her that a part of Speaking Rain was already gone from them—and this time Kaya was the one to be left behind.

Tee-tew! Was that a bird call? Glad to be distracted from her painful thoughts, Kaya looked over her shoulder. Two Hawks had taken a flute from his bag and had played those sweet notes on it. Looking pleased with himself, he held out the flute for Kaya to examine. This flute was longer and more finely crafted than the first one he'd made. And when he put it to his lips, he could play a melody.

They all listened to Two Hawks play the soft, beautiful song. Then his father laughed and said something to White Braids that made her laugh, too.

"What did he say?" Kaya asked her sister.

As Kaya watched them work,
her own feelings were as tightly twisted as the cord.

Speaking Rain leaned close. "He said that when he was young, he could play love songs well because he got so much practice!" she whispered with a smile. "He says that soon Two Hawks will be old enough to serenade the girls as he once did."

Kaya studied her friend. He was no longer the angry, stubborn, skinny boy who'd crossed the Buffalo Trail with her. He was taller, his shoulders were broader, and his dark eyes were clear and bright. She realized with surprise that someday he would be a handsome young man. She wanted to tell him that she liked the tune he played, but suddenly she was shy. Instead, she took Speaking Rain's doll and with her finger showed her sister where she'd mended it.

Outside the tepee the storm howled, but inside it was dry and warm. When it was time to sleep, White Braids spread deer hides on both sides of the fire. Two Hawks and his father lay down on one side. On the other side, Speaking Rain lay on her bed of hides next to the old woman's. "Here's a place for you beside me," she said to Kaya, as though everything were just as it had always been. *Except that everything's different!* Kaya thought.

Kaya lay down and tried to sleep, but she was troubled and restless. She felt the familiar warmth of her sister's shoulder against her own, but in her heart she was cold and lonely. *Creator, spare my life from accidents, illness, and loneliness,* Kaya prayed silently. *Help me to face life with a strong will and without fear of man or beast—or change.*

Chapter Four
A New Path

By the time Kaya and Tatlo were taken across the river the next morning, everyone was already at work. Kaya found her mother kneeling on a smooth rock, cutting the head off a large salmon and taking out the entrails, which she put into a basket to take to the trash heap. Kaya knelt beside her and used her hands to speak over the roar of the falls. *Speaking Rain is alive! She's over there!* Kaya pointed at the opposite shore.

Eetsa sat back on her heels, and her eyes filled with tears. It was a long moment before she could answer. *We'll cross the river tonight and bring her back,* she signed. *Go tell your grandmother!* She pointed toward the workplaces on the hillside.

Kaya found Kautsa on an upland rise, spreading salmon eggs to dry on tule mats. Here the smell of fish was especially strong. Attracted by it, bald eagles and condors circled overhead, riding the winds. The roar of the falls wasn't so loud on this side of the rise, and Kaya didn't have to shout to tell her grandmother about Speaking Rain.

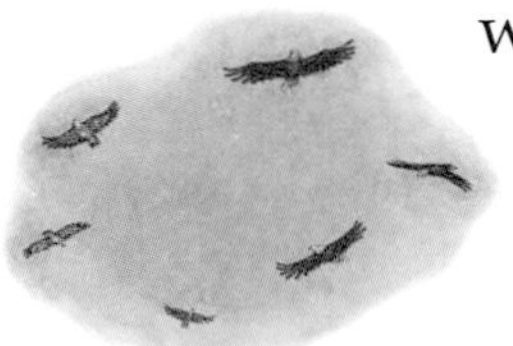

Kautsa clasped Kaya's hand when she heard that Speaking Rain was alive. "I've hoped and prayed to hear this!" she said. "Tell me what happened to her after you two were separated."

Careful not to leave out anything, Kaya told all that had happened to her sister and about her life now with White Braids.

When Kaya was through, Kautsa handed her a basket of salmon eggs. "Hold this while I spread these eggs. When they're dry, you can have some for yourself to trade. Maybe you can get some beads, or a shell to hold them while you're working."

Kaya knelt in silence by her grandmother for a little while. Then she said, "Speaking Rain's different now, Kautsa."

"Do you mean she's grown?" Kautsa asked.

"She's a little taller, that's true, and her face is rounder," Kaya said. "But she's grown inside. She seems older. I always looked out for her. Now she doesn't seem to need my help anymore."

"If she can't see, she'll always need some help," Kautsa said. "That hasn't changed, has it?"

"She's still blind in her eyes," Kaya said. "But her heart sees things clearly."

"Everything you're telling me is good news, but you look troubled," Kautsa said. "Didn't you sleep well, Granddaughter?"

Kaya bit her lip. "I stared at the fire all night," she admitted. "But that's not what troubles me. Speaking Rain told me about an important vow she made, one she won't break, no matter what."

"A vow she refuses to break?" Kautsa asked. "Her spirit is strong, then. All that she's been through has made her that way. What was her vow?"

"She vowed she would never leave the woman who saved her life!" Kaya blurted out. "Because of that, she can't live with us anymore!"

Kautsa looked at Kaya long and hard. "Aa-heh, your sister is very strong. But listen to me, Granddaughter, you have strength, too."

"Do you mean the strength I needed to escape from the enemies?" Kaya asked.

"Not exactly," Kautsa said. "I mean you have the strength to make hard choices."

"Are you telling me I should let Speaking Rain go?" Kaya asked.

"I'm not telling you that at all," Kautsa said. "You wanted your sister to live. Don't you want her to have the life she chooses?"

"But I want her to choose to live with me!" Kaya said. "With us! I would miss her so. You'd miss her, too, Kautsa!"

"Aa-heh, I would miss her very much," Kautsa admitted. Her face was grave, and she looked sad. "Remember how you wanted Lone Dog to stay with you? But it wasn't her nature to do that. Perhaps now Speaking Rain must follow her own path—just as you must follow yours."

The heat shimmering up from the stones and the smell of the fish made Kaya dizzy. She swayed, and Kautsa clasped her shoulder, then handed her the water basket so that she could drink. "I know you love your sister," Kautsa said gently. "You love your parents, and all your grandparents, and Brown Deer, and the twins—and others. You love many people. So does Speaking Rain. If she loves and respects two mothers now, she has her own hard choice to make. Do you understand me?"

Kaya wiped her lips on her wrist. "Aa-heh," she murmured.

Her grandmother patted Kaya's shoulder. "You need to rest," she said. "Brown Deer is working near the tepees. Stay with her for a while. She'll want to hear about Speaking Rain, too."

Kaya found Brown Deer kneeling in the shade of a tepee, pounding dried salmon into fine pieces in a stone mortar. Kaya sat down next to her sister and hurriedly told her all about Speaking Rain.

"I have split feelings," Brown Deer admitted after Kaya had told her everything. "One feeling is happiness that our sister is alive and well. The other is sadness that she won't live with us."

"Aa-heh, I understand," Kaya said right away. "It's just the way I feel about your hope to marry Cut Cheek," she went on, surprised to hear herself confessing these feelings, too.

"But you like him, don't you?" Brown Deer asked, startled.

"I *do* like him," Kaya said. "And I know you love each other. I want you to marry. But at the same time, I don't want to lose you. So I'm happy and sad at the same time."

Brown Deer set down the stone pestle and put her hand on Kaya's arm. "We'll always be sisters, no matter what happens. You'll never lose me, I promise. Now we should think about how we can help Little Sister with her choice."

Kaya scrubbed at her eyes with the back of her hand. Brown Deer's kind words helped ease the ache in her chest. "I just wish there was some way for Speaking Rain to choose *both* Eetsa and White Braids!" she said.

Brown Deer scooped the ground-up salmon from the mortar and put it into a basket lined with dried fish skins. "We're friends with the Salish," she said. "We trade with them, and we join them to hunt buffalo. White Braids could live with us for a time. Is that what you mean?"

"White Braids doesn't speak our language—I don't think she'd want to leave her own people," Kaya admitted. Then she sat up straighter. She wasn't tired anymore—and she had an idea. "But

"We'll always be sisters, no matter what happens."

Speaking Rain knows both languages now. Maybe she could go back and forth between White Braids and us."

"What do you mean?" Brown Deer asked. She stopped working and looked closely at Kaya.

"I mean, what if Speaking Rain chose to live part of the year with White Braids and part of the year with us?" Kaya said. "That way she could keep her vow to help White Braids, but she wouldn't have to give up our family completely."

Brown Deer's eyes lit up. "That's a new path to think about—a girl shared by two families and two tribes. We'll have to ask Kautsa for her counsel. But first I must finish this. Crane Song will be coming to check on me, and I still have so much work to do. Look, the sun is almost high overhead."

That evening Kaya and her parents tied up the canoe on the far shore and started walking upstream toward the Salish village. Eetsa carried a large woven bag filled with dried kouse roots to give to White Braids in thanks for saving her daughter. "I've told you how Speaking Rain came to be our child, haven't I," she said to Kaya.

Kaya hurried to keep up with Eetsa and Toe-ta. "We were both still babies, weren't we," she said. She'd heard this story many times.

"You'd learned to walk," Eetsa said. "And Speaking Rain had just taken her first steps when her mother grew sick and died. Her mother was my dear, dear cousin. We'd grown up together, and when we both gave birth to daughters, we became closer still. When Speaking Rain lost her mother, and her father was gored to death on a buffalo hunt, Toe-ta and I took her to raise."

"But at first Speaking Rain didn't like you," Kaya added. "When you went to pick her up, she tried to squirm out of your arms!"

"She couldn't see me, but she knew from my touch that I wasn't her mother, so she fought me," Eetsa said. "When she hit me with her little fists, I thought, 'Tawts! She's a strong one! She'll be an independent girl.'"

"And you loved her anyway," Kaya said.

"I loved her *more* for that strong will of hers!" Eetsa corrected her.

"Now Kautsa's told us that Speaking Rain's

made a vow she won't break," Toe-ta said. "That's her strength showing itself."

"But she can't leave us!" Kaya insisted. "Maybe she can live with White Braids—and with us, too. Do you think she'd do that?"

"We've talked that over with Kautsa," Eetsa said with a frown. "But live with two families? That troubles me."

"We'll hear what Speaking Rain has to say," Toe-ta said firmly.

As they approached the Salish tepees, Kaya saw Speaking Rain standing near the path. Her head was tilted as if she could hear their footsteps approaching, and she was smiling. Kaya's heart lifted all over again to see her sister looking so healthy and well. "We're here!" Kaya called out.

Eetsa hurried to her daughter and hugged her tightly. "I feared for you!" she exclaimed. "And how I missed you! Now you're back again!"

Not saying a word, Toe-ta picked up Speaking Rain. She put her arms around his neck while he held her tightly against his chest for a long time. Then he set her gently down. White Braids, Two Hawks, and Two Hawks' father waited a few paces away. With his hands he thanked White Braids for saving his child's life, and he thanked Two Hawks and his father for bringing them together again.

"White Braids has prepared a meal for you," Two Hawks said. "Come to our tepee with us."

White Braids opened the tepee flaps to let in the cooling wind. As they sat there, shadows lengthened and the evening star began to rise. With Two Hawks interpreting, the talk was slow and respectful, and there was much to say. Kaya watched Speaking Rain's face as she turned first toward one speaker, then toward another, as if she were reaching out to them all.

Finally Toe-ta said gently, "Little Daughter, you haven't said much. What are your thoughts?"

Speaking Rain swallowed hard, and she sat up straighter. "Toe-ta, before you came here tonight, I told White Braids I'd made a vow always to help her, as she's helped me. 'We need each other now,' I said. She argued with me—she wants me to go back to you. But I can't break my vow. I owe her my life. You understand, don't you?" She turned to face White Braids and repeated what she'd said in Salish.

Right away White Braids spoke with her hands,

I love this girl very much, but I never wanted to take her from you! I only wanted her to live, to be well, to join her family again!

I believe you, Eetsa signed to her. *But I also respect my daughter's vow and her need to keep it.*

Kaya could hold back no longer. Putting her hand on Speaking Rain's, she said, "Listen to me. I have an idea." Then slowly, carefully, she described how Speaking Rain could spend part of the year with White Braids and part with her own family. "If you do that, you can choose *both* of your mothers. Do you think that's possible, Little Sister?" As she spoke, Kaya heard her heart like a soft drumbeat, urging *Find a way, Find a way.*

"Do you mean go across the river with you for a few days, then come back here to join White Braids again?" Speaking Rain asked. "I could do that, but what would happen when the salmon fishing ends and we all leave the Big River?"

"Consider this," Toe-ta said. "You could go with us to Salmon River Country for the winter. Then, when it's digging time, we could take you back to the Palouse Prairie."

"You could meet White Braids there for the hard

work of the digging season," Eetsa added.

Two Hawks spoke a moment with his father. "My father says some of my people can meet you at the Palouse Prairie, then bring you here to the Big River again."

"Everyone will help," Kaya said.

Finally Speaking Rain said slowly, "I can follow the path you've shown, Sister. I believe I can keep my vow but not hurt anyone. That's more than I ever hoped!"

"Then you'll come to us now?" Kaya asked her sister.

"Aa-heh," Speaking Rain said. "Katsee-yow-yow, Kaya."

When White Braids put her wrinkled hand on Speaking Rain's shoulder, Kaya knew she, too, was saying *Katsee-yow-yow.*

Kaya got to her feet. She was so light with relief that she felt like floating up to the small clouds racing toward the setting sun. "I'll carry your things, Sister. Let's go now while it's still light. The others want to welcome you back, too."

A few days later, Kaya was walking with Speaking Rain to their tepees when she saw people gathered on the plain upstream from the falls. The fishermen caught only as many salmon as the women were able to clean—when they'd caught their limit, they got together for games, trading, and races. Now Kaya saw a group of men sitting in two lines facing each other, playing the Stick Game. They were drumming to distract the ones trying to guess which hands hid the small bone markers. They kept track of the score with sticks stuck upright in the ground. A few women stood behind the players, singing loudly to add to the confusion. Jokes and shouts and songs echoed across the valley.

"I hear so much commotion!" Speaking Rain said. "They're playing the Stick Game, aren't they? Let's join them."

"But some riders are getting ready to race their horses," Kaya said. "Let's go there instead. I'll tell you everything that's happening with the races!"

They hurried toward the long, flat stretch where riders raced their horses. Kaya loved to watch the beautiful horses run, though it made her ache for Steps High. As she came closer, she realized that one of the riders on his spotted stallion was Cut Cheek. Brown Deer stood on the sidelines with some other young women. She had the twins with her.

"Is Cut Cheek going to race?" Kaya called as she and Speaking Rain came up to them.

"A band from the prairie challenged us!" Brown Deer said. Her eyes flashed with excitement. "They bet us that their best horse and rider could beat our best horse and rider. Our men chose Cut Cheek."

"I hear his stallion's fast!" Speaking Rain said.

"But look at that gray horse the other man is riding!" another girl said. "Those long legs, that sleek head! They say he's as swift as an antelope."

"But Cut Cheek's horse runs like a cougar!" Brown Deer said. "And Cut Cheek is a better rider, so he's sure to win. You'll see!"

The two men rode away from the others toward the far end of the race grounds.

"Cut Cheek's horse is straining at the bridle as if he can't wait to race!" Kaya told Speaking Rain. "The gray horse is prancing and snorting. He's ready to run, too!" Kaya held her breath as the starter raised his arm and brought it down. "There they go!"

Both horses leaped forward like arrows shot from bows. The riders lay low, their faces close to their horses' necks. The horses lengthened out, running faster with each stride, their tails streaming. Cut Cheek and his horse seemed to blend into a single being, running easily, as if they could race forever.

"Cut Cheek's ahead!" Kaya said. "He's pulling away from the gray! They're coming to the finish line!"

"Cut Cheek wins!" Brown Deer cried out.

"I want to ride like he does!" Wing Feather cried.

"Nimíipuu won the bet!" Sparrow hopped around like a jackrabbit.

As the riders rode back slowly, cooling their horses, Brown Deer waited, smiling. Kaya knew her sister was struggling not to let her feelings show, but her face shone.

"You're proud of Cut Cheek, aren't you!" Kaya said.

"Aa-heh," Brown Deer said. "He rode well! But I have something else to be happy about. Just before I came to the race, Crane Song nodded at me!"

"Was her nod a good sign?" Kaya asked.

"It was only a little nod," Brown Deer admitted.

"But it must mean she's pleased with you," Speaking Rain assured her.

"At least a little pleased!" Brown Deer said. "I'm so glad! Would you two look after the twins for a while? I want to tell Cut Cheek—he'll be glad, too. I'll work even harder now!"

"Aa-heh, go tell him," Kaya said, giving Speaking Rain's hand a squeeze. "We'll take care of these bothersome little brothers of ours!"

As long as the run of salmon continued, Kaya helped Speaking Rain go back and forth across the river, staying a few days at a time with each of her two families. Now the season for fishing on the Big River was nearing an end. Speaking Rain would travel with Kaya and her family to higher country for berry picking and hunting, then down to Salmon River Country before snows came. But first there was work to be done while the men completed their fishing.

Kaya knelt beside Brown Deer under a tule mat lean-to they'd made on the hillside above the river. Speaking Rain sat beside them, a box-turtle shell filled with green paint in her hands. Brown Deer had soaked a buffalo hide in the river and had staked it onto the ground in the shade. Now she was going to paint a design on the hide so that she could make it into a parfleche.

"Remember, we have to work quickly so the hide won't dry out. Paint bonds only to a damp hide," Brown Deer said. "I'll lay out the shapes and outline them. Kaya, you help me fill in the larger spaces with paint."

The tule mat shelter they'd made was a small one, but Tatlo managed to creep into its shade. Kaya scratched him behind his ears, and he went to sleep with his head on the edge of her dress.

Brown Deer had already covered the damp hide with a clear mixture of fish eggs to make it smooth and waterproof. Now she laid peeled willow sticks on it in a design of lines and triangles. She dipped a buffalo-bone tool into the paint, then expertly traced the design she'd made, drawing the edge of the bone tool down the hide in long, steady lines.

Kaya dipped in another tool, letting the porous

bone soak up the lovely green paint made from river algae. Then she began spreading it where Brown Deer showed her.

"White Braids told me that soon she'll go back to her home country," Speaking Rain said. "I'll be sad to see her go."

"She's a fine woman to adopt you in this way, and you'll meet her again at the Palouse Prairie in the spring," Brown Deer said.

"Will Crane Song be coming with us for the berry picking, or will she go back to Cut Cheek's family when we leave?" Kaya asked her older sister.

Brown Deer's lips turned up a little as she drew. "Crane Song told me this morning that she'll be leaving us." She sat back and looked hard at the lines she'd made, then dipped her tool in the paint again. "She said I must work hard even when she's not around to keep an eye on me. But she told me she's satisfied I'll make Cut Cheek a good wife!" She sighed deeply, as if she'd been holding her breath for a long time.

"That's wonderful news!" Kaya exclaimed. "Why didn't you tell us?"

"I was afraid it might not be true," Brown Deer admitted.

"But it is!" Speaking Rain said. "I hear it in your voice. You're almost singing today."

"I feel like singing," Brown Deer said. "Cut Cheek said his parents will join us soon. They'll visit our family with their gifts. Then, in a little while, we'll visit them and give them ours. I'm making this parfleche for Cut Cheek's mother. I want it to be my very best work!"

"You've already made so many gifts," Kaya said. "Woven bags of beautifully dyed cords and grasses, and baskets filled with dried roots."

Brown Deer set aside her tool and picked up

a little buckskin bag of powdered pigment. She took the container of green paint from Speaking Rain and gave her a large mussel shell in its place. "Hold this for me now," she said. "I want to mix up some red."

Speaking Rain held the mussel-shell bowl steady in her cupped hands as Brown Deer mixed the dry paint with water. "What will happen next?" she asked.

"First, Cut Cheek will live with us for a while," Brown Deer said. "Crane Song says he has to show my parents he'll be a good provider." She took two fresh bone tools from her kit and let them soak up the beautiful red paint, the color of sacred power.

"And when he proves himself?" Kaya asked.

"Then we'll make our home with my family for a time," Brown Deer said. "In hunting season, my parents will need our help more than Cut Cheek's family will. So I won't have to leave you now, after all." Her gaze caught Kaya's, and they both smiled.

"Soon you'll plan your marriage," Kaya said. The words were good ones.

Tatlo's paws twitched in his sleep—he was chasing rabbits in his dreams. Kaya stroked his warm head as she watched paint seep into the bone tools. She'd thought she would lose Brown Deer when she married, but that was not to be. She'd thought Speaking Rain would leave them forever, but that wasn't going to happen, either. If only she could get her horse back, her life would be complete. As she picked up her bone tool, she felt as if her full heart were glowing like the crimson paint.

A Peek Into the Past

Summer in 1764

In Kaya's time, and for many generations after that, a girl almost could have walked across the river on the backs of salmon nearly as large as she was!

During *wa-wama-aye-khal*, the season when salmon reach the canyon streams, the Columbia River came alive with a parade of color and shimmering movement as millions of salmon swam upstream. Nez Perces gathered to fish with thousands of other Indian people at Celilo Falls, a series of thundering waterfalls, boiling rapids, and churning narrows on the Columbia River.

Nez Perces, like all the Indian peoples who fished at Celilo, believed that the salmon chose to swim upstream every year

Women cooked salmon by threading sharp roasting sticks through the fillets and planting the sticks so they leaned over a low fire.

and give themselves to humans. They respected and thanked the salmon for choosing to make the journey. Nez Perces also believed that Salmon People lived in a great house under the sea. When it came time to run up the river, the Salmon People took the form of fish. After they died, their spirits returned to the great house under the sea. The Salmon People could then take their fish form again, and make the journey the following year.

The first time young fishermen dipped their nets into the roaring river in search of salmon, they learned that nature was a force far more powerful than humans. Salmon were so big and so strong that, even when they swam against the ferocious current, they could pull a fisherman into the rapids. According to Nez Perce legend, a beautiful maiden lived inside Celilo Falls. Sometimes she would sacrifice fishermen to the river, as a way of giving back to the salmon. The river would give, and the river could take. It was a fair trade.

Fishing technique has stayed the same since ancient times.

Celebrating the salmon was celebrating the cycle of life, and it was amazing to be a part of it. Each year, Nez Perces watched full-grown salmon surge upstream to lay eggs before they died. The largest falls in Celilo were over 20 feet high, and it was an awe-inspiring sight to see the huge fish leap and lunge their way to the top. Sometimes they fell, but they never gave up. In the autumn, young fingerling salmon ran downstream, racing to start their new lives in the sea.

For thousands of years, Celilo Falls was one of the greatest trading sites on the whole continent. People came from as far away as modern-day California, Alaska, and Missouri. From the mouth of the Columbia River, coastal people brought ocean fish and rare dentalium shells. People from the Cascade Mountains brought soft blankets woven from mountain goat hair. Great Plains people brought buffalo robes and dried meat. Nez Perces were especially proud to bring their fine horses, wintered in the mild valleys where they had plenty of

At Celilo Falls and other gathering places, family shields were displayed next to tepees.

Horse collars were used only for sacred ceremonies in Kaya's time, when people paraded their horses in honor of their ancestors.

Children and adults played Shinny, a game like field hockey.

fresh grass to eat to keep them swift, strong, and beautiful. Every group of people had its own beautiful artistry to share—baskets, bags, wood and stone bowls, painted hides, and jewelry and other adornments.

Summer at Celilo was the most festive time of the year, with thousands of people feasting, dancing, parading, racing, and gaming. The most popular game was the Stick Game. Two teams knelt and faced each other. One player hid a bone in each hand. One bone was marked, while the other was plain. Players on the other team had to guess which hand held the unmarked bone. Counting sticks were used to keep score.

At night, the drumming would begin, and young people gathered for courtship dances. Most marriages were arranged by parents or grandparents, but some parents paid attention to their sons' and daughters' choices. After

During the Stick Game, crowds of people gathered behind the players, singing and joking to throw off the players' concentration.

A courting couple in 1903. In Kaya's time, marriage to a person in another tribe was good for trading, and meant less warring and raiding, too.

the dances, a young woman might hear the sound of a flute outside her tepee. That meant a young man had come to court! If a Nez Perce youth married into another tribe, those families became trading partners. It was good to have a trading partner from another tribe, because the two partners probably would have different goods to trade.

courting flute

Celilo Falls remained a vibrant place to celebrate Indian life and culture until the 1950s, when the United States government decided to build The Dalles Dam. The dam would flood Celilo Falls, stopping its mighty flow so a hydroelectric plant could harness the power of the water to make low-cost electricity.

Indian chiefs spoke out against the dam. They told government officials how they depended on the salmon to live. They reminded officials of the Treaty of 1855, which said that their tribes kept the right to fish at their usual and accustomed places, specifically Celilo Falls. Women elders spoke too, telling of previous broken promises and pleading with the officials not to repeat those mistakes.

Girls might trade dolls, jewelry, bags, belts, or even moccasins with trading partners their own age.

The wild waters of Celilo Falls boomed like thunder.

On March 10, 1957, Congress closed the gates of The Dalles Dam, and the people of many tribes gathered to watch their ancient fishing sites slowly disappear under the flood.

The salmon's survival is now threatened. Eight federal dams have been built between the streams where salmon are born and the ocean where they live as adults. In Kaya's time, millions of salmon swam in the streams and rivers. Today, only a few thousand make the journey upstream to lay their eggs.

The Creator put the Nez Perce people where salmon return, and they and all of the other tribes who share these waters are committed to protecting this place. They are working to have four of the dams partially removed to help the salmon return to the streams. Just as the mighty salmon still struggle up the waterfalls, the Nez Perce people will never give up.

GLOSSARY OF NEZ PERCE WORDS

In the story, Nez Perce words are spelled so that English readers can pronounce them. Here, you can also see how the words are actually spelled and said by the Nez Perce people.

Phonetic/Nez Perce	Pronunciation	Meaning
aa-heh/'éehe	*AA-heh*	yes, that's right
Eetsa/Iice	*EET-sah*	Mother
Hun-ya-wat/ Hanyaw'áat	*hun-yah-WAHT*	the Creator
katsee-yow-yow/ qe'ci'yew'yew'	*KAHT-see-yow-yow*	thank you
Kautsa/Qáaca'c	*KOUT-sah*	grandmother from mother's side
Kaya'aton'my'	*ky-YAAH-ton-my*	she who arranges rocks
Nimíipuu	*Nee-MEE-poo*	The People; known today as the Nez Perce Indians
Pi-lah-ka/Piláqá	*pee-LAH-kah*	grandfather from mother's side
tawts/ta'c	*TAWTS*	good
tawts may-we/ ta'c méeywi	*TAWTS MAY-wee*	good morning
tee-kas/tikée's	*tee-KAHS*	baby board, or cradleboard
Toe-ta/Toot'a	*TOH-tah*	Father

wapalwaapal	*WAH-pul-WAAH-pul*	western yarrow, a plant that helps stop bleeding
wa wama aye khal/ waw' ama' ayqáal	*wah-wah-mah-eye-KHAL*	the season when the salmon reach the canyon streams to spawn; August

The Books About Kaya

MEET KAYA • An American Girl
Kaya's boasting gets her into big trouble
and earns her a terrible nickname.

KAYA'S ESCAPE! • A Survival Story
Kaya and her sister, Speaking Rain, are captured in
an enemy raid. Can they find a way to escape?

KAYA'S HERO • A Story of Giving
Kaya becomes close friends with a warrior
woman named Swan Circling, who inspires
Kaya and gives her an amazing gift.

KAYA AND LONE DOG • A Friendship Story
Kaya befriends a lone dog, who teaches her
about love and letting go.

KAYA SHOWS THE WAY • A Sister Story
Kaya is reunited with Speaking Rain, who has
a surprising decision to share.

CHANGES FOR KAYA • A Story of Courage
Kaya and her horse, Steps High, are caught
in a flash fire. Can they outrun it?

Coming in Spring 2003
WELCOME TO KAYA'S WORLD • 1764
History is lavishly illustrated with
photographs, illustrations, and artifacts
of the Nez Perce people.